MY BODY, MY BRAIN

THIS BOOK BELONGS TO:

___

From one neurodivergent mother, for her kids, and all the kids – N.G.

For Nore, Kobe, Fien & Fijs – love I.D.

With thanks to Emma-Rose Parsons of Spectrum House.

Scholastic Press
An imprint of Scholastic Australia Pty Limited
(ABN 11 000 614 577)
PO Box 579 Gosford NSW 2250
www.scholastic.com.au

Part of the Scholastic Group
Sydney · Auckland · New York · Toronto · London · Mexico City · New Delhi · Hong Kong · Buenos Aires · Puerto Rico

Published by Scholastic Australia in 2024.

A catalogue record for this book is available from the National Library of Australia

ISBN: 978-1-76152-462-2

Typeset in Might Could Pencil Regular and Fink Heavy.

Inge Daniels created these illustrations digitally.

Printed in China by RR Donnelley.
Scholastic Australia's policy, in association with RR Donnelley, is to use papers that are renewable and made efficiently from wood grown in responsibly managed sources, so as to minimise its environmental footprint.

10 9 8 7 6 5 4 3 2 26 27 28 29 / 2

A Scholastic Press book from Scholastic Australia

MY BODY, MY BRAIN

Nicki Esler Gill & Inge Daniels

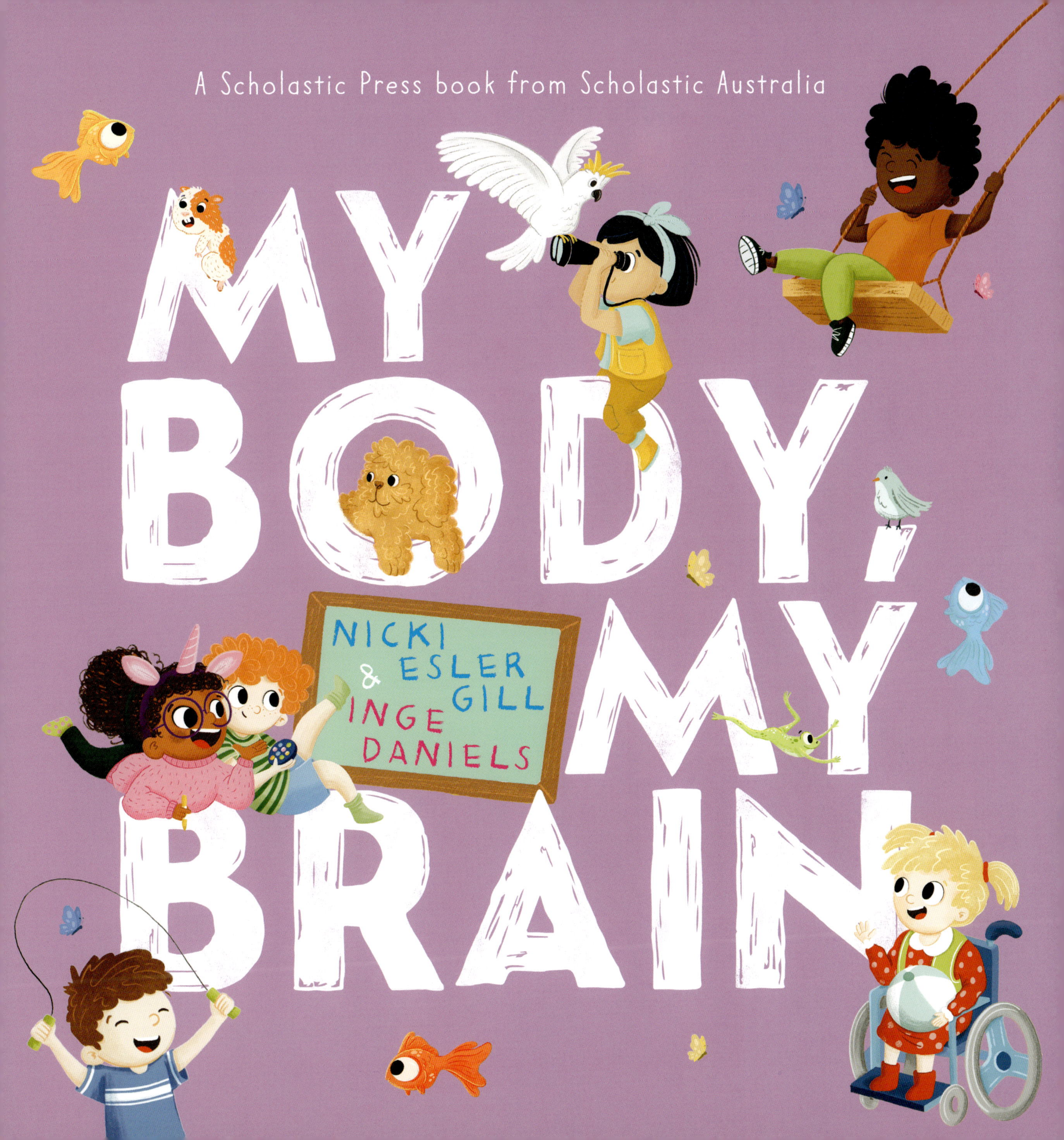

Have you ever been a **chatterbox,**
with lots of things to say?

Or has it seemed your voice
has left and gone on **holiday?**

Have you ever had a favourite **sound**
that helps you feel at rest?

Have you **sung** or **hummed** or **whistled?**
Moved to music you like best?

Have you stayed **still** as a statue
and as **quiet** as a mouse
when it's mat time or it's nap time
or for movies at your house?

Have you found that quiet's **tricky**
and your body wants to move,
and that **fidgeting** is helpful
when it's not time to groove?

Have you ever been with lots of friends and not known where to **look?**

Have you ever felt more **comfortable** with one friend or a book?

Have you spent the day **high-swinging,**
spinning, tumbling, giving chase?

Or **snuggled** in a blanket
in a quiet, cosy place?

Have you ever tried to **listen**
when the teacher talks in school,

but your brain has gone **adventuring**
somewhere you thought was cool?

Have your feelings felt so **stormy**
that they **tumble** you about?
Have you learned the things that help
you **ride** the stormy feelings out?

Just like our bodies differ,
you can look around and see
that our brains are **different** too
and that's the way it's **meant to be!**

When something's
easy for your friend,
but **difficult** for you,

and you're feeling **sad**
or **worried**, like you
don't know what to do,

remind yourself you're **good** at
things that other kids find **hard**.

Think of the **frog** and **goldfish**
in the fishpond in the yard . . .

The fish breathes **underwater**.
It can swirl and swim all day.
The fish looks up at lily pads.
It sees the world **one way**.

Life's **fun** beneath the surface,
but the fish is **unaware**
that from up above the lilies
there are flowers **blooming** there!

The reason Frog can see them
is her different set of **skills** –
she's good at jumping, breathing air
and swimming without gills.

If she **worried** over all the things
a goldfish brain could do,
she might miss the **lovely** froggy
things she does, and so would you!

Imagine you were planning
an enormous birthday bake
but you only had some **flour**.
Do you think you'd make a **cake?**

You need **butter!** You need **sugar!**
And lots of **sprinkles,** yum!
When **mixed,** these make a
scrummy cake and very happy tum.

With people it's the **same.**
(I'm not saying that we're cake!)
But that different brains are **needed**
for the **world** we want to make.

We all are the ingredients
for making life that's **sweet.**
Our difference is important.
It can even be a **treat!**

Some brains give **super senses.**
Might their owners make perfume?
Some brains think best in **nature.**
Watch them help our gardens bloom!

Some brains love to **organise** and know the plan each day.

And others love **surprises,** painting, dance and messy play!

Life's not a **competition,**
or a whose-brain's-better test.
We all have strengths and challenges.
We all can do our **best.**

We all can make someone feel
they're **welcome** and **belong**,
and you can know you're welcome too,
and difference makes us **strong**.

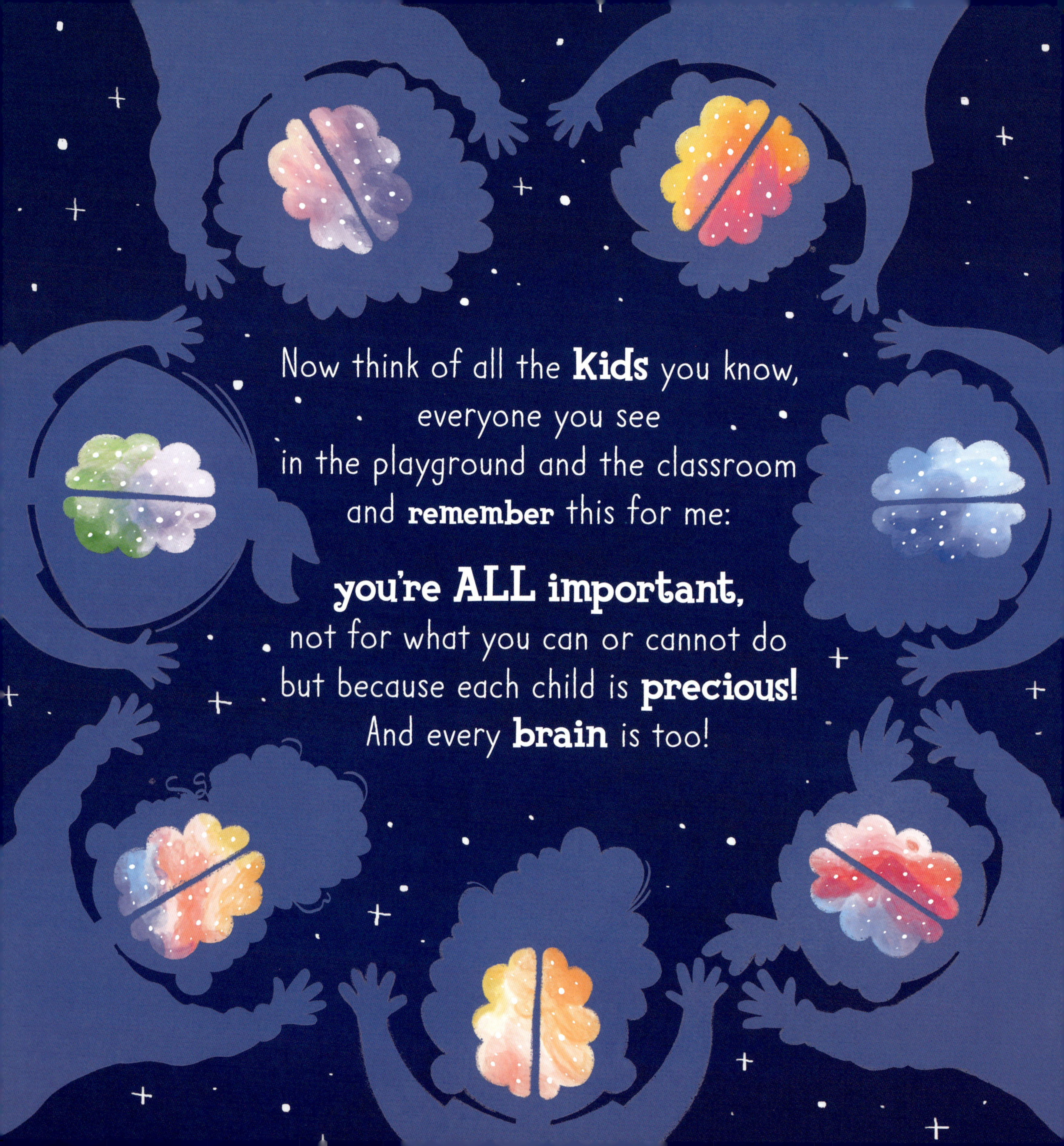

Now think of all the **kids** you know,
everyone you see
in the playground and the classroom
and **remember** this for me:

you're ALL important,
not for what you can or cannot do
but because each child is **precious!**
And every **brain** is too!